MW01711711

THROWAWAY CHILD

ELISE ABRAM

EMSA PUBLISHING

Throwaway Child
Copyright © 2012 by Elise Abram
Copyright © 2014 by Elise Abram
Copyright © 2017 by Elise Abram

All rights reserved.
Published by EMSA Publishing 2017
Thornhill, Ontario, Canada

This book is sold subject to the condition that it shall not, by way of trade or otherwise, be lent, resold, hired out, or otherwise circulated without the publisher's prior consent in any form of binding or cover other than that in which it is published and without similar condition, including this condition being imposed on the subsequent purchaser.

No part of this book may be reproduced, stored in a retrieval system or transmitted in any form or by any means electronic, mechanical, photocopying, recording, or otherwise, without the prior written permission of the publishers, except by a reviewer who may quote brief passages in a review to be printed in a newspaper, magazine or journal.

The final approval for this literary material is granted by the author.

Third printing
This is a work of fiction. Any similarity between the characters and situations within its pages and places or persons, living or dead, is unintentional and coincidental.

Printing History
First Edition: December 2012
Second Edition: August 2014 with *The Mummy Wore Combat Boots*
Third Edition: August 2017

PUBLISHED BY EMSA PUBLISHING
http://emsapublishing.com

Throwaway Child is printed in Garamond.

Credits: Cover artist: Joel Abram

ALSO BY ELISE ABRAM

The Nexus and Other Stories
The New Recruit
I Was, Am, Will Be Alice
The Revenant: A YA Paranormal Thriller with Zombies
Phase Shift
The Mummy Wore Combat Boots

FOREWORD

Throwaway Child was first published in 2012. At that time, the world had yet to bring the issue of Native residential schools to the forefront. Since then, apologies and monetary restitution have been made to many victims of the Canadian residential schools, but the psychological wounds will be slow to heal if they heal at all.

The report by the Truth and Reconciliation Commission of Canada alluded to on the back cover, "documented horrific physical abuse, rape, malnutrition and other atrocities suffered by many of the children who attended the schools, typically run by Christian churches on behalf of Ottawa from the 1840s to the 1990s."[1] In his speech to the Assembly of First Nations Special Chiefs Assembly, Prime Minister Justin Trudeau conceded that "residential schools and other decisions by governments were used as a deliberate tool to eliminate Indigenous languages and cultures."[2] He has since asked

---

[1] *Justin Trudeau pledges reconciliation in Canada after Aboriginal Abuse*. The Guardian. December 15, 2015. https://www.theguardian.com/world/2015/dec/15/justin-trudeau-pledges-reconciliation-canada-aboriginal-abuse

[2] Trudeau, Justin. *Prime Minister Justin Trudeau's Speech to the Assembly of First Nations Special Chiefs Assembly*. December 6, 2016. http://pm.gc.ca/eng/news/2016/12/06/prime-minister-justin-trudeaus-speech-assembly-first-nations-special-chiefs-assembly

the Pope to apologize for how the Catholic residential schools treated their students. A Global News report states the Pope "seemed open to the idea."[3]

I first learned of Canadian residential schools in a second-year university course[4] on issues in Indigenous education, and I had no idea of the dirty little secret that was Canada's residential schools.

In 2017, at the time of this book's third publishing, it seems unreal that someone like a police detective would be unaware of the existence of residential schools. Rather than look at the story as being unrealistic, I ask you to suspend your disbelief as you travel back to 2012 (or thereabouts) with me for the duration of this story.

I hope you enjoy reading *Throwaway Child* as much as I did writing it. It certainly is an eye-opener!

Elise Abram

---

[3] Smith, Joanna. *Justin Trudeau presses Pope for official apology for residential schools*. May 29, 2017. http://globalnews.ca/news/3485515/justin-trudeau-pope-official-apology-residential-schools/

[4] At the risk of aging myself, I took the course in or around 1987.

1

The frontal bone is the first to crown through the thick dirt. It gleams bright white in the glare of the halogen lamps.

"I think it's a skull," my wife tells me, sickened. Forensic anthropology was never her bag. Human remains can be kind of messy. She much prefers the tidy theory of Cultural Anthropology, but this site came my way on short notice, and I didn't have enough time to put together a proper crew. I got her to come by promising she'd find nothing more than bones picked clean by nearly half a century's time. For some people, even that's a little too much to stomach.

I rub her back across the shoulders, hoping it'll calm her. "Are you okay to finish the excavation?"

She smiles, nods, and continues digging.

Ten minutes later she calls me over again.

"It's small," she says, matter-of-factly.

"Probably a child's."

She winces. "A child's?"

I nod.

"Oh, God. How old?"

A few more trowel strokes and I'm able to free the skull from its resting place.

"Judging by the number of milk-teeth?" I turn the skull first this way, then that, in an effort to calculate a ratio of baby teeth to missing teeth to new growth. "Seven. Maybe eight."

"Eight years old?" she asks. "Boy or girl?"

"Hard to tell. Skeletal structure's hard to differentiate at that age." My wife stares at the find, paling.

"Molly, are you okay?" I ask her.

She stares at the skull and remains mute.

"Molly?"

When she looks up at me, her expression is drawn. "Fine," she says, standing. "I need some air." She drops her trowel on the ground. It slices at the soil as it lands.

"She okay?" Detective Constable Michael Crestwood, my contact at the local police department, says.

I tell him she's fine. Maybe a little claustrophobic, but fine. I think it was the fact the skeleton she found belonged to a child that's jarred her more than anything else. We've been trying to get pregnant without success for almost a year now. It's the notion that anyone could think of something as precious a child as throwaway that's gotten to her. It's knowing someone was fortunate enough to have been gifted the care of an innocent life, abused the responsibility, and buried his sin in an unmarked grave in the basement. It's feeling hopeless, because even if you could prove who committed the atrocity in the first place, it's probably too late to do anything about it.

"Richardson?" Crestwood asks. "Are you okay?"

"I think I need some air, too."

2

Crestwood was the one who'd call me in late last night. Acting on a tip they'd received on the CrimeStoppers call line, police raided an old Victorian mansion turned crack-house near the downtown core. They'd imported Vinnie the "Cadaver Dog" from Britain, a Springer spaniel trained to sniff out buried human remains. Vinnie went crazy atop the concrete basement slab. I arrived during the final stages of its removal.

My name is Palmer Richardson. I teach archaeology at the University of Toronto in Ontario, Canada. My specialty is forensic anthropology. I'm like those guys you see on television who work alongside the police to identify murder victims, especially when all that's left are the bones. Virtually everything a person does in life leaves its mark on the bones. Things like sex, age, diet, physical activity—it's all there, written in the bones. The trick is in learning how to read the signs. Crestwood had been on enough of these cases to know when something's been buried like that and for such a long period of time, chances are nothing'll be left behind but the bones. He'd called me relatively early in the investigation so I'd be on-call the moment they needed me. I usually keep my wife out of things like this—Molly gets squeamish cleaning chicken—but I needed the extra set of hands.

Crestwood stands inside the screened-in porch. "You guys okay out here?" he asks. We mutter something sounding like affirmation. "'Cause we've found some more, if you're ready for it."

Molly and I look at each other. She still looks a little green, even bathed in the glow of overcast sunlight. "You don't have to finish this, Moll," I tell her.

"If it were my child, I'd want to know," she says. "That child's mother has a right to know."

3

I bring the skeleton back to the lab to get started on identification while the police continue to dig. Crestwood said he'd call if they found any more remains, and I promised I'd call once I had an identification.

There are a lot of variables going into the identification of remains through craniofacial reconstruction, most the result of human error during measurement. Tissue depth is another problem. Without knowing nationality, cultural identity, or sex, the reconstruction is nothing short of my best guess. Even so, at the very least, I can produce a depiction which is a good approximation of what the person might have looked like whole. If I'm lucky, it'll be close enough for a loved one to notice.

There are two schools to facial reconstruction: two-dimensional computer simulation and three-dimensional clay reconstruction. I took art and sculpting classes to master the skill of clay reconstruction and so I do both in my practice—the clay reconstruction first, and then the two-D computer reconstruction as a check. The police and public then have two representations of the deceased. Hopefully one gets ID'd.

To do the three-D craniofacial reconstruction, small, rubber markers are placed on bony landmarks on a mould of the skull to denote skin and cartilage thickness according to known averages. Then clay is layered on, first to represent the facial muscles, then the skin. The process takes the better part of two weeks for me to finish. When I'm done, I'm left with a young child with slightly feminine, possibly Native American features. The computer reconstruction confirms it: a First Nations female child, features so similar to my reconstruction, they might almost be twins. The greatest divergences between the two are the lips and ears; I've never quite been able to master lips and ears.

I'm putting the finishing touches on the reconstruction—skin pores, eyelashes—when Crestwood pays me a visit. He enters the lab and makes a bee-line for the girl's skull. "Don't take this the wrong way, Richardson, but what you do creeps me out."

I join him in admiring the reconstruction. Sometimes what I do creeps me out, too. I rotate the reconstruction so I can see the eyes. They look a little crossed.

"The reason why I'm here," Crestwood says, still fascinated with the girl's face, "DNA testing confirms the child's female." He picks up the Polaroid print of the reconstruction on the counter. "May I?"

"You'll want this, too." I hand him a colour printout of the two-D computer reconstruction. "She's Native. First Nations. Dentition indicates she was around eight to ten years of age."

"That makes things a whole lot simpler." He opens a file onto the counter and shows me a list. "The basement floor was cemented over in the early sixties. Sixty-two, maybe sixty-three. There are twelve possibles, girls of about the same age living at the home around that time. Four of them of Native descent.

"I'm heading over to the east end to question one now."

"Keep me posted, will you?" It looks like one of the eyes has shifted in the socket ever so slightly, and I work toward righting it.

I hear Crestwood hesitate on his way out. "Want to ride shotgun?"

"Really?"

"Really. Yeah. It's that mug of yours. That and all of your...professor suave sophistication that gets people to talking."

That translates to Crestwood wanting me to play good cop to his bad. "So, you want me for my body, then."

"Something like that, yeah."

4

Mary-Catherine Ramsey is a waitress in a diner in Toronto's east end. The regulars huddle over the bar, beer in hand, talking to the bartender while ESPN plays on the flat-screen. They seem oblivious to the fact this is the middle of a workday. Seniors and businessmen enjoy grease-laden main courses whilst seated round red-plaid, plasticized table cloths. The smell of stale beer mingled with burnt grease and dampness pervades the atmosphere. Crestwood and I hesitate in the foyer until a hunched-over man in a white polo shirt, old enough to be my father, beckons us to enter. He seats us and hands us stained menus.

Crestwood waves off the menus with his badge. "Mary-Catherine Ramsey?"

The man nods, knowingly, an expression that indicates the trouble he's had with this particular member of his service staff. He grumbles something and takes his leave. A few moments later, an attractive, Native American woman in her late forties or early fifties, wearing dark slacks and a white polo shirt approaches. Her name tag reads "Mary-Cate".

"Mary-Catherine Ramsey?" Crestwood asks.

"Yes," she says, tentatively.

"Ms. Ramsey, I'm Detective Constable Michael Crestwood, Metro Toronto Police." He flashes his badge once more, and nods at me. "Dr. Palmer Richardson, Forensics. We'd like to ask you a few questions, if we may."

"What's this about?" she asks. Her chocolate brown eyes moisten and I can tell: she's terrified.

"Do you recognize this person, Ms. Ramsey?" He hands her the Polaroid of the finished reconstruction and the blood drains from her face. She sits down.

"Oh, my God. It's Essie." She stares at the picture, stroking the cheek in the photo with the tip of her finger.

"Essie?" Crestwood asks. He pulls the list of residents from his jacket pocket and voraciously searches for the name. "There's no record of an Essie living in the home at that time."

Mary-Cate sniffles. "Her name was Samantha. We used to call her Essie because she always wore a big S on her blouses. Her mama did that for her before she came so she'd be sure to come back with the right clothes.

"Is she okay?"

Crestwood consults his list once more. "Samantha Keenlyside," he says.

"Mary-Cate—pick up," the old man shouts from the kitchen entryway.

Mary-Cate ignores him. "You haven't answered my question," she says.

"She's dead," I say, softly. I hate this part of the ride-along. "Your friend's dead." I look down at my hands in my lap. "I'm sorry."

"Essie's dead? How?"

I see the owner approach through the corner of my eye. "Pick up, Mary-Cate," he says, standing behind the woman.

"This is police business, sir," Crestwood informs him as if he didn't already know. "Ms. Ramsey will be there for her pick up when we're done."

The old man utters an indignant huff and shambles away.

"How. Did. She. Die?" Mary-Cate asks through her tears.

"We don't know yet," I say.

"Ms. Ramsey, when was the last time you saw Essie?"

"We were young. Real young." She takes a napkin from the dispenser on the table, blows her nose with it, and crumples it into a small ball. "Eight, maybe? Nine?"

Crestwood makes note of this in his pocket notepad. "And what happened then? Why did you stop seeing each other?"

The old man returns with three cups of coffee and a small plate of creamers. "Take as much time as you need," he tells Mary-Cate.

"Essie ran away," she says as soon as the man creeps off.

"You know that for a fact?"

Mary-Cate nods. "We always talked about it, running away to find our parents. I just figured Essie got tired of waiting for me to get up the courage to go with her. I got adopted not too long after that so I never knew if she ever came back. I keep looking for her, like on the Internet, you know? Hoping I'll find her one of these days. Essie and me were close. Like sisters. I miss..." A small sob escapes from deep inside her throat. "I miss her," she says in a quiet voice.

I take her hand. "I'm sorry for your loss," I tell her.

5

Samantha Keenlyside's original address is a First Nations Reserve about two hours north-east of the city. It's still relatively early in the afternoon, so I go along to keep Crestwood company.

It's almost dinner-time when we arrive. Crestwood flashes his badge at the first person he sees and asks for directions to the Keenlyside residence. The man he asks points to a trailer at one end of a circular driveway. A sign indicates this is the Community and Guest Services Centre. A man dressed in blue jeans, a jean jacket, and plaid shirt meets us as we exit Crestwood's unmarked car. He wears a baseball cap drawn low over sunglasses which he removes to examine Crestwood's badge.

"Keenlyside, eh?" he says, as if trying to remember. "There used to be a Marjorie Keenlyside lived with her father and child a few decades back. She shacked up with the eldest Cattroll boy, seven, maybe…ten years ago. If I'm thinking of the right person, you can find her down the street, make a left, fourth trailer down."

6

Marjorie Keenlyside answers the door when we knock. Crestwood introduces us and she invites us in. She lives modestly, as I assume most do on the reserve. The trailer is dark and decorated sparsely, yet tastefully. Floral-printed curtains frame the small windows. We sit at a chipped, melamine tabletop in the kitchen area. Marjorie offers us tea and arrowroot cookies.

She doesn't recognize the girl in the Polaroid when Crestwood first shows it to her. "You have a daughter, ma'am? Samantha?"

"I do, but that doesn't look like her, not at all."

"Do you know where Samantha is now?"

She shakes her head and sighs. "I haven't seen Samantha since she was six years old."

"Why is that, ma'am?"

I take a hasty sip of tea and burn the roof of my mouth.

"I think I have a photo of my daughter somewhere." She excuses herself and disappears into the bedroom. We hear papers shuffling as she speaks. "It won't take but a minute to find." She returns a moment or two later with a portrait of a small girl, fine hair in pigtails splayed out above her ears like sparks from a firecracker. She's smiling in the photo and holding a grey stuffed animal with a plastic snout, quite the contrast from the morose child with the thick, black, Cleopatra-style hair of my reconstruction.

Marjorie holds the two photos—the one of the reconstruction side-by-side with the one of her daughter—and examines them. Slowly, a look of realization passes over her features and silent tears fall from the corners of her eyes. "It's her, isn't it?" she asks.

I find police business fascinating, my drive-alongs with Crestwood invaluable, but the one part about it I never get used to is informing people of the passing of a loved one. You'd think, in my line of work, being so close to death—what with identifying human remains and all—I'd get used to it. No matter how many times I tag along, witnessing the onset of the grieving process never gets any easier. "I'm so sorry for your loss," I tell her, and I am. Genuinely sorry. We had a miscarriage a few months back. And while it's not the same, I can identify. All the planning. All the hope. All the dreams. I don't care what the pro-choice people say—almost from conception, that baby was a part of our lives, a member of our *family*. Losing the *idea* of a child is pretty near every bit as sorrowful as losing an actual child.

Crestwood tries to refocus her by asking, "Ms. Keenlyside, when did Samantha enter foster care?"

"She was six when they came."

"They?" I ask.

She blows her nose into a white handkerchief with baby pink embroidered flowers. "Government workers," she says as if swearing. "They came regularly to make sure we were taking care of our own. As if we wouldn't do it without their say so.

"One day, they gave us a list of problems. Told us our homes weren't fit for our children. They were small and dirty. Said we weren't feeding the children properly and that they were sickly because of it. They told us they would work with us to get our children back as soon as possible."

Marjorie sniffles and then laughs once, hard and breathy. "The social worker came once a month for a few months after that, mostly to complain. She complained about the mess, so I cleaned it up for the next time, and she complained about the empty cupboards. I was one person—what did I need a full pantry for then?

"I borrowed money the next time so my pantry would be full when the time came. And then she complained I needed a job. Where did she expect me to get a job? It's not like there's a lot of places I can get to without transportation.

"I worked something out with the Cattrolls. One of them'd take me to work in the morning and one of them'd bring me home at night. For a price. I got a job at a nearby diner. The next time the social worker came, she made a big deal about that Samantha didn't have her own room, and I would have to move.

"Where did she expect me to go? I was lucky enough to have a roof—any roof—over my head." She downs a gulp of tea and I do the same. Even cold, it does the job of washing the cotton from my mouth.

"She came once or twice after that, but my situation never changed." Marjorie wipes the tears from her eyes with the heel of her palms, then snorts a laugh. "'History is doomed to repeat itself'," she says.

"I'm sorry?" says Crestwood.

"I heard it somewhere. History repeated itself again." She looks at us as if we're supposed to understand. When it's clear we don't, she rolls her eyes and says, "The government stole me from my mama and then it stole my baby from me.

"When the social worker came for me to sign papers so's the girl could be adopted, I signed. It's just as well. I'd've been a shitty mother anyway, raised in the residential school like I was. Wouldn't have even recognized my own Samantha on the street if I bumped right into her." She picks up the photograph of Samantha, aged six, the one with the firecracker pig-tails. "Samantha," she wails. "My baby."

7

I wasn't there with Molly when we lost the baby. She'd stayed home from school that morning, feeling under the weather, and I'd gone in to teach a class. I'd called to check on her when I arrived on campus and again in the moments prior to the lecture. She was fine, she'd said, was about to lie down and have herself a nap. An hour into the lecture, my T.A. barged into the theatre, so winded he could barely speak. When at last he was able to fill his lungs and speak, it was as if he'd stolen the breath directly from *my* lungs. Unable to reach me, Molly'd called the department secretary who, in turn, dispatched my T.A. The ambulance was on its way and I was to meet her at Toronto's Mount Sinai Hospital. Almost twenty minutes had elapsed since her call.

In no shape to drive, I hailed a cab to the hospital. Molly lay on a cot in fetal position, clad in layered gowns, and covered with a thin white sheet and thermal blanket the colour of buttercups. The smell of blood, sour and coppery, hung in the air.

When she saw me, she just stared. Tears began flowing from her eyes. The ones from her left eye trickled down over the bridge of her nose, some falling into her right eye, others following the curve of her nose, all of them making the pillowcase damp. "My baby," she'd said, much the same as Marjorie Keenlyside, fraught with self-loathing, as if she'd neglected to do the one thing that could have prevented the situation, and then she apologized.

8

Crestwood invites me for a bite and a beer when we get back to Toronto. I call Moll and have her meet us there. While we're waiting for the appetizers to arrive, we fill her in on the case.

"We never learn, do we?" she says without skipping a beat. "We *are* doomed to repeat ourselves; it's human nature."

"What do you mean?" Crestwood asks her.

"Marjorie Keenlyside."

Crestwood says nothing. The waitress sets a gigantic plate of nachos in front of us, and my mouth starts to water. Up until this moment I hadn't realized just how famished I really was.

"Her people?" Molly says.

Crestwood says nothing while I crunch down on a nacho dripping with chili and covered in cheese.

"What the first Europeans did to North America's Aboriginal population is obscene. Disease. Genocide. Don't even get me started on the residential schools."

"Marjorie Keenlyside said she'd been raised in a residential school," Crestwood says.

I take a sip of cold beer from a frosted mug, the first sip since this whole baby thing started. Daunted that it hadn't happened for us in the first few months, Molly put us both on a health-food diet, something about beer affecting sperm count and the possibility of toxins and antibiotics and such being passed on to the baby or other.

Molly plays with the paper sleeve from her straw while she speaks. "The Europeans infantilized the Natives, deemed their religion heathen, stole their children and warehoused them in the residential schools where they suffered corporeal punishment if they so much as thought an Aboriginal thought, or whispered their native tongue, even amongst themselves."

"What's she talking about?" Crestwood asks me.

"You didn't know?" I ask. Crestwood shakes his head. He doesn't know. Few people do. They take an affront to the so-called benefits Canadian native populations have—no taxes, reservation land, special hunting privileges...What they don't realize is they've earned it. Hell, they've more than paid for it with the blood and tears shed after generations of (some would argue) criminal governmental misconduct. The truth is, we owe our Aboriginal population so much more than compensation. What the first settlers did to them was nothing short of physical genocide. Later generations, from about the turn of the century to as late as the sixties or eighties, continued the abuse into cultural genocide. They stripped those people of who they were and then condemned them when so many turned to the bottle—or worse—to deal with the abuse. "You are in for one hell of a history lesson, my friend." I signal for the waitress to bring him another beer.

"Inside the residential schools the children suffered all kinds of abuse, including beatings, just for speaking their own language," Molly tells him.

"When they were released from the residential schools, they had nowhere to go. They considered themselves Christians, but were shunned by the rest of society because they weren't Caucasian. They might have returned home, but they were shunned by them as well because they were strangers, even to their own parents, taught to believe those that still practiced the old ways would burn in hell. No family, no money, no job, no home—"

"When was all this supposed to have happened?" Crestwood asks as he pops a nacho.

"At least into the middle of the last century."

"You mean the nineteenth century?"

Molly shakes her head. "No, I mean the twentieth century."

"No way."

Molly takes a sip of her soda water and smiles knowingly.

"Why would people do this? Send their children to these schools?"

"It was institutionalized," Molly tells him, "the law." I love to see the flame ignite in her eye when she's impassioned with a cause. I want to grab her, hold her, feel her body tremble with indignation against mine. Instead, I take her hand from across the table and squeeze.

"The police frequently assisted in the taking of these children, as if they were under arrest," she continues. "If you were working near one of the reserves, you might be compelled to take some of these children away from their parents as part of your job, Michael."

"You guys're shitting me, right? No way that happened here."

"No shit, my friend," I say, "no shit." The waitress puts a beer down on the table and I slide it over so it's in front of Crestwood. "I thought you could use another."

People seem to have this glorified idea about Canada. It's said we are welcomed abroad; our neighbours to the south, not so much. We have fewer guns and less crime than them, as well. Canada never had slavery. We're considered peaceful neutrals, like the Swiss. Canada's a cultural mosaic, where everyone, no matter their heritage, is welcomed. The truth is, Canada is not unlike any other country in the world. We like to think we never had slavery, but we did, we just ended it earlier than in the south. The frequency of violent crime is on the rise. Canada stayed out of the so-called 'War Against Terrorism', but just until new residents took up on Parliament Hill. And for a long time, the tile in our cultural mosaic that was Canada's aboriginal population was kept hidden, a dirty little secret that's only just in recent decades been brought forth into the light of day.

"The government treated its native populations as if they were children," Molly continues. "Thought they weren't able to raise their own as contributing members of society. Within a single generation, that became a self-fulfilling prophesy."

"What do you mean?" Crestwood asks.

"I mean the Keenlysides—Marjorie and Samantha both—didn't stand a chance." She takes a long sip from her soda.

"Marjorie was doomed from the start," I say. "Taken from her parents, locked away in an institution, probably suffering long-term abuse—"

"And then going back to the reservation and having a daughter of her own," Molly says, "never having been properly parented and having no idea how to parent, the cycle of neglect starts all over again—"

"Until the government intervenes once more," I say, "taking Marjorie's child from *her*, locking *her* away—"

"Only Samantha wasn't as lucky as Marjorie to survive the ordeal," Crestwood adds.

"Samantha wasn't as lucky," Molly reiterates. She excuses herself and runs to the restroom.

"Kind of taking it hard, huh?" Crestwood asks of her once she's gone.

"She's nothing if not passionate," I say, not wanting to get into the whole baby dilemma thing. Not with Crestwood. Not now.

9

Two days later, Crestwood tells me they've located the social worker assigned to the Keenlyside case all those years ago. She lives midtown, in a convalescent home. He lets me tag along for the ride.

Gloria Parsons is nearing her eightieth birthday. The staff uses a wheelchair to help her get around. Her hair and skin are greyed. Her teeth have a yellow tint. Only her eyes, bright and blue, belie her age. Gloria doesn't remember Samantha, per se. "There were so many Indian children," she tells us, "too many. Our orders were the same. Go to the reserves and find things, find problems."

"You were actually told to find reasons to take their children?" Crestwood's still adjusting to the knowledge that the system he's sworn to serve and protect is capable of such gross injustice.

"It wasn't like that," she tells us. "Not like that at all."

"What *was* it like?" Crestwood sounds angered, indignant.

"The Indians lived in a ghetto. What could they teach their children? How to hunt? Fish? A lot of good that would do them.

"Most of those children were living in squalor when I took them—"

"Not Samantha Keenlyside. She had a mother who loved her. A mother who did whatever you asked so she could keep her child and make it right," Crestwood says.

"I gave them a chance for a better life."

Crestwood, a quick study, says, "You gave them the tools to perpetuate a cycle of self-destruction."

I put my hand on Crestwood's shoulder. It seems to have a calming effect. He turns toward the window in the room and looks out in silence.

"Mrs. Parsons? Ma'am?" I say, taking a stab at it. "If you could just take another look at this picture, maybe something will come to mind." Mrs. Parsons takes the photo, a copy of the one Marjorie Keenlyside had cherished for all these years, and studies it. A slow smile forms on her thin, dark lips.

"This girl. I remember this girl. Sad story, this one is."

"How so?" I sit at the table beside her and lean toward her as she speaks.

"She came to us looking like this, all smiles and stray hair. She had old eyes—they looked like they'd already lived a lifetime. She was at the institution for two years before she disappeared.

"She had a friend, another girl. The two were inseparable until just before the end. She was supposed to be adopted, this girl was. The adopting couple came for a visit a few weeks running, even had her stay overnight one weekend, to acclimatize her to her new surroundings.

"Then there was a fight, a horrible fight. Between this girl and her friend. Both were bloodied and blue by the end of it. We had to separate them. The next day the couple came to pick her up and she was nowhere to be seen. We searched the place high and low and still came up empty. The couple went home empty-handed, the poor would-be mother crying so hard, the husband told us she had to be sedated.

"The girl never turned up. We figured she was a runaway—"

"Did you report it to the police?" Crestwood asks, still looking out the window.

"I'm sorry?"

He turns and nears the woman, his girth towering over her, threatening. "Did you report it to the police? The girl—her name was Samantha, by the way, Samantha Keenlyside. You used to call her Essie."

Mrs. Parsons is silent.

"It's a simple question, really: Did you report Essie as a runaway?"

"No. We didn't," she says quickly. "The police were never notified."

"An eight-year-old child, a baby, goes missing, and you don't report it to the police?"

Mrs. Parsons looks down at her gnarled hands writhing in her lap. "It wasn't procedure. Indian kids went missing all the time. Either they turned up or they didn't."

"Well, Essie turned up, all right." He opens a folder he's been holding and drops it on the table in front of Mrs. Parsons. "This is what Essie looks like today."

Mrs. Parsons barely glances at the photographs of Samantha Keenlyside's remains and tears begin to well in her eyes. "I...I...I'm sorry," she says. "I didn't know."

"You didn't *care* to know," Crestwood tells her. He gathers the photos back into the folder and turns as if to leave.

"One thing, Mrs. Parsons, and then we'll leave you be," I say. "The couple. The one that was going to adopt Samantha. You wouldn't by any chance remember their name?"

"As a matter of fact, I do. It was Ramsay. Like that chef on T.V."

10

Crestwood and I make a beeline for the bar in north-Toronto, the one where Mary-Cate Ramsay works. We catch her as she's coming off her shift. She looks at us, nods knowingly and leads us to a booth near the kitchen entryway.

"You never told us about the circumstance of your adoption, Ms. Ramsay," Crestwood says.

"I told you I was adopted—"

"But not in lieu of Essie."

Mary-Cate's mouth opens as if she's about to say something, then, having uttered nothing, closes.

"How fortuitous Essie chose to run away when she did. Otherwise, you might have lived out the rest of your childhood locked away in that place."

"It wasn't like that," Mary-Cate says, "not at all."

"It was bad, wasn't it, Mary-Cate," I say, hoping to sound sympathetic. "There was abuse, wasn't there?"

Mary-Cate sniffles and nods her head.

"And loneliness. I'll bet it was lonely. I'll bet you missed your parents, didn't you?"

She lets out something that sounds like a whimper. I pull some serviettes from the dispenser and hand them to her. "It felt like I was in jail. I was six-years-old when they took me. Six! The police showed up on my doorway and pulled me from my mother's arms. I remember her calling to me. Calling my name. To this day, I hear it in my dreams. That sound, the sound of desperation, of despair, calling my name.

"At the home, we were beaten regularly. If we forgot ourselves and spoke in the language of our fathers, if we questioned their religion, if we hummed our songs to ourselves. I was six. What did I know?

"When I met Essie, it was like I'd found my soulmate. We spent each and every day there protecting each other, nurturing each other, helping each other to keep our true selves hidden from our captors.

"And then she was going to be adopted. She was going to leave me. I was going to be alone again."

"And so you fought," Crestwood says.

"We had a fight. I loved Essie, and I thought she loved me, like a sister, but even sisters fight sometimes, don't they? Children can be cruel, even to family, can't they?

"She was awful. Told me I was jealous, that I wasn't good enough to be adopted, that I was still too Indian to ever be loved by anyone.

"She said it like it was a swear word: *Indian*. I was a proud Cree. My parents taught me to be proud of my heritage, like their parents before them. Said the white man tried to steal their culture away from them but they wouldn't succeed. Told me I had to learn the old ways so I could teach it to my children when the time came.

"Essie and I used to meet in the basement and I would teach it to her. The language—what little of it I knew, how to dance…In many ways, my heritage was my security blanket. When I sang Cree songs, I remembered my family, and I felt loved. And I felt worthy of being loved.

"When the Ramsays first picked her, Essie told me she couldn't be a part of it anymore, learning the ways of our ancestors. She said if I insisted on keeping with the old ways, she couldn't play with me anymore. The longer the Ramsays courted her, the more I knew she meant it, and I would eventually lose her.

"We had a fight about it the night before she disappeared. In the playground. Beat each other but good.

"The next day she was gone."

"Gone?" Crestwood asks. "Just like that?"

Mary-Cate nods wryly.

"The Ramsays stayed away for a few months and then they came back. They knew me because Essie and me were friends. I guess that's why they picked me. Because maybe I reminded them of her.

"They were different. Essie thought she had to hide who she was because of them, deny her heritage, but she was wrong. The Ramsays embraced my heritage. They made sure I remembered what it meant to be Cree. Essie was wrong, and we fought for nothing." Mary-Cate looks at her hands, shredding the paper napkin on the table. "It was all for nothing."

Crestwood opens his mouth as if to speak, but I beat him to the punch. "What was for nothing, Mary-Cate?"

She says nothing in reply.

"Mary-Cate? You said it was all for nothing. What was?"

She looks like she wants to tell us something, like she's ready to speak, but she remains silent instead.

"What was all for nothing, Mary-Cate?"

"All the arguing. All the fighting." Mary-Cate bites her lower lip and blinks away some tears. She sighs and says, "Essie's death."

Mary-Cate hides her eyes with one hand. "Oh, God. Essie didn't have to die, not like that."

"Like how, Mary-Cate. How did Essie die?"

"Like you showed me. Buried. In the basement."

"How did she *get* buried, Mary-Cate?"

She closes her eyes and sobs. "I don't know."

"I think you do, Mary-Cate. Think hard. Back to that night. The night before Essie was supposed to leave with the Ramsays—"

"We fought," she says. "Screamed. No one heard us. No one went into the basement. That's how we knew it was safe. To remember our heritage. That night. I was in the basement remembering the ways of our ancestors as my mother had taught me, when Essie arrived. She wanted to say goodbye; I wanted no part of it. We argued and then fought some more. I..." Mary Cate closes her eyes to expel some tears. When she opens them and continues to speak, she looks away from us. "I pushed her. She hit her head on the wall. Fell to the ground. Wouldn't wake up. I went to get help, but I knew I'd be in for a beating if they knew what I was doing there, in the basement.

"I got some ice instead. Held it to the gash on her head.

"I spent the night in the basement with her, nursing her. We weren't missed.

"The next morning, the Ramsays arrived after breakfast. Nobody noticed Essie was gone until then. I rushed to the basement to wake her, but she was cold. I think it wasn't until that very moment I realized she was dead and that I'd...I'd..." Mary-Cate looks at me through the corner of her eye and then looks away again. "I buried her. It was tough. The ground was hard. It took a few days.

"Later, when the Ramsays returned, they asked for me. It was like everything was okay, like Essie had sent them for me because she couldn't go, like she was telling me she forgave me."

Crestwood sighs before speaking. "The Crimestoppers call?"

"It was me," she says. "I heard they'd raided the old orphanage and thought about Essie. I swore to myself I'd never forget her, my little sister who died so I could have a better life. It embarrassed me that I'd forgotten. I knew they'd cemented over the old basement floor. They'd never find her if they didn't know where to look. I thought it was time. She deserves better than an unmarked grave in a crack-house basement."

Mary-Cate blows her nose, takes a deep breath, and sits upright against the back bench seat of our booth. "I think I'm ready now, to pay for what I've done. It feels good to be free of the burden I've been carrying about her death."

Crestwood looks at me as if trying to gauge my opinion on the matter. Mary-Cate Ramsay was as much a victim as Samantha Keenlyside. Mary-Cate was just a child when Samantha died. Samantha's death was an accident. Already feeling as if she were in prison, what terror might her young mind imagine *real* prison to be like? Mary-Cate must have panicked at the though of going to jail, any eight-year-old would. I feel badly for Mary-Catherine Ramsay. I'm glad I'm not the one who has to decide her fate.

"Am I under arrest, Detective?" Mary-Cate asks.

"I'll need you to come to the station for questioning," Crestwood says in a low voice.

"You were a child when it happened," I tell her. "Essie wasn't killed out of malice. You've already suffered a lifetime for your sin."

We walk Mary-Cate out to Crestwood's car. He puts her inside and closes the door. "Why do you always have to do that?" he asks. "Smooth things over."

"Imagine the hell that girl must've suffered her whole life. She needed someone to give her absolution."

"That's what priests are for. And juries."

"I have only two words for you, my friend," I say, "sensitivity training."

Crestwood laughs and shakes my hand. "I'll keep you posted," he tells me.

11

Once at the station, Crestwood took Mary-Cate's statement. He promised to try to keep her name out of the press. Upon closer examination, there proved to be a small dent at the back of the occipital lobe of the skull. Minor blunt trauma. Not enough to seriously compromise the skull structure, but probably enough to cause a hell of a concussion. It's possible Samantha Keenlyside's brain bled out as a result of the trauma, eventually leading to her death, which backed up Mary-Cate's story. Due to her age of maturity at the time of the incident, chances were Mary-Cate might not be charged with the crime, or so Crestwood thought. The Crown attorney had yet to weigh-in on the matter.

I went back to the campus to teach my last class of the day. When I return home, it's to find Molly had lit enough tea-lights in and around the dining room to burn the house down if we weren't careful. Empty red and tan paper bags with black Chinese characters from our favourite take-out are on the kitchen table. Molly finishes emptying the contents of the last container into a bowl from our good china collection as I enter the room.

I hug her from behind and kiss her neck where it meets her shoulder. "Chinese take-out, huh?" I say. "What's the occasion?"

"Not now," she says. She takes me by the hand and leads me to the dining room table, which is covered with a black tablecloth. The plates gleam bright white in contrast to the dark tablecloth. She opens a bottle of sparking peach cider and pours some for each of us in crystal wine glasses from the china cabinet.

"I want to propose a toast," she says. "To poor Samantha Keenlyside, may she rest in peace.

"To Mary-Catherine Ramsay, may God be with her and give her strength over the next few months.

"And to us.

"Palmer, I'm pregnant."

THE FURTHER ADVENTURES OF
MOLLY AND PALMER IN...

THE NEXUS

AND OTHER STORIES

Aliens, ghosts, the paranormal, a glimpse at a possible future...

There are more things in heaven and earth than modern man will ever know or understand.

The Nexus

They say be careful what you wish for. Meet Josef Schliemann, noted expert in pseudo-archaeology who sponsors a dig beneath a historic church in downtown Toronto. Said to have been built on a tract of land sacred to prehistoric Indigenous peoples living the in the area the secrets of the site have been lost to time. Will Josef survive when he finds the object of his desire?

A Morgan by Any Other Name

In a future where cloning has been perfected—sort of—Rachel, a Morgan model, should have the world at her feet, but she's not happy. What is the one thing a teenage clone desires?

At the Mere Thought Of

What happens when your worst nightmare comes true? Businessman Crane is about to find out.

The Circle of Life

Bob wakes up the night after attending a wild rave to find he's not himself. He wakes up, buried alive, and hungry…for flesh.

One book, thirteen stories.

In The Nexus and Other Stories, science fiction author Elise Abram explores the myths of the modern world.

THE FURTHER ADVENTURES OF MOLLY AND PALMER IN...

PHASE SHIFT

If you knew the world was about to end, what would you do?

If you found the key to another Earth, would you use it?

When archaeologist Molly McBride finds the key to a doppelganger Earth she is swept into a world of conspiracy that could end in the death of not one, but two planets.

Will Molly be able to prevent the impending cataclysm?

THE FURTHER ADVENTURES OF PALMER AND MICHAEL IN...

THE MUMMY WORE COMBAT BOOTS

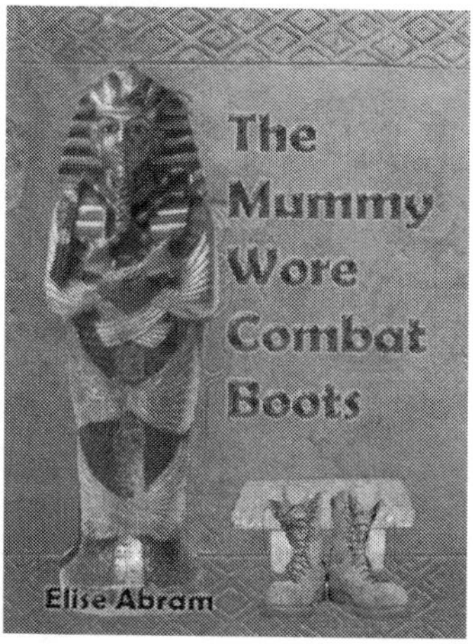

When called to investigate an uncatalogued sarcophagus found in storage at the Royal Ontario Museum, forensic anthropologist Palmer Richardson has his work cut out for him. When the mummy inside proves to be that of a teenage boy, Palmer joins Detective Constable Michael Crestwood of the Metropolitan Toronto Police. in an investigation delving into the world of online gaming where losing health points in a skirmish could have serious implications for a player's life in the real world.

Inspired by real-life headlines, THE MUMMY WORE COMBAT BOOTS highlights the growing divide between children who live their lives immersed in a digital culture and the adults tasked with raising them who live in the real world.

75242579R00024

Made in the USA
Columbia, SC
16 August 2017